Diary of a High Class Prostitute

Scarlett Series Book 1

By: Kristin Michelle Adams

Dedication

I would like to dedicate this book to all my readers. Thank you all for your support.

January 1st, 2014

    I can't believe after all this time I am finally starting a diary. This diary was a gift from my sister on Christmas. I don't even know where to begin. I guess the beginning is where most people start. So, here I go.

    My name is Monica Cox, and yes that is my real last name, but I go by Scarlett because of my long red hair and green eyes. I am a twenty four year old high class prostitute, better known as a female escort. Before you start judging me, listen here. I didn't grow up in a broken home or anything.

    My parents are actually perfect. My mother is a middle school history teacher, and my father is the principal. Yep, as lame as it gets. So, how did I end up being a prostitute you ask? Well, ever since I lost my V-card my freshman year in high school at the tender age of fifteen, sex has been a massive part of my life. I just can't help it. I love it!

    Yep, I love plain old vanilla and hot rough sex. I like to mix it up with girls, and I love it when I have more than one to play with. I guess you can call me addicted. That is why I decided to become a prostitute, escort, call girl or whichever term you would prefer to use. What better way to get all the sex I want, and hell, I get paid for it. I guess you can call it my dream job.

Now, I know what you must be thinking. What about STDs? Well, that is the beauty of being a high class girl. Every John I have has to have papers proving he or she is clean of all STDs. I get tested monthly to prove I am also clean.

The other thing you might be wondering is what about pregnancy? Well, I have all of that covered as well. In fact, all of Joe's girls are covered. That's my boss by the way. I have been on the Depo-Provera shot since I was eighteen. I have been on it so long that I no longer have periods, which is amazing by the way.

Like I said, Joe is my boss. I know most people think the pimp is a horrible man that treats women like shit. But, Joe isn't like that. He truly cares what happens to his girls. In fact, if Joe was ever interested, it wouldn't take much for me to truly become his girl. Problem is, Joe doesn't swing that way.

Yep, you got it. I probably have the one and only gay pimp. Now, this doesn't mean he isn't strong or anything. If there is ever a problem, Joe always takes care of it. Last week my best friend, Candy (that is her prostitute name), was hit across the face by her John. Joe ended up beating the shit out of the guy, and the John is no longer able to buy one of his girls again.

As for me, I have never had a John hit me when I didn't want to be hit. If you get what I'm saying. I have had my share of rough Johns and Janes. Janes are just what I call a female John. It just doesn't sound right to call a female a man's name.

To be honest, I don't get too many Janes. Once in a while, I have the occasional John that brings his wife to have a threesome, or for her to have a first time lesbian experience. Other than that, not too many lesbians ask for my services.

Now, you are probably wondering if I'm bisexual. Well, it's hard to say. I truly don't think so. I have sexual experiences with women because it's part of my job, and I get paid extra for it. Do I get off on it? No, I really don't. I love dick! All kinds: big ones, short ones, some as thick as my arm. Yes, those do exist.

I also have a huge collection of sex toys. Most of my toys are used only once, and then I toss them. I do keep my glass toys no matter what, unless they are chipped, since they can be put in a dishwasher and sanitized. Now, for all those soft flexible toys, those get tossed. I don't want any bacteria lingering around. For a prostitute, I am kind of germ-a-phobic. The way I think of it is I do whatever it takes to make sure I stay healthy and clean.

Besides, with the web pages like Amazon and EBay, I can buy sex toys at wholesale cost. Also, a good thing about online shopping is I don't have to worry about looking like such a slut. Like I said before, I love sex.

Anyway, the reason I decided to start writing today is because it is New Years day. I figured New Year, new start. Besides, I wanted to write down every detail of my night with my John.

At three o'clock, I got a text from Joe stating I was going to meet my new John at the Art Museum in town for a fundraiser, and I was to dress up. I looked at the details and saw I was to meet him out front at six pm. As my John already knows what I look like from pictures, I wasn't concerned about finding him. I started to get giddy at the prospect of getting dressed up.

It's not every day I feel like Julia Roberts in Pretty Woman. I rushed around my apartment trying to decide what to wear. Do I go with the simple black dress or my favorite emerald green satin dress that hugged my curves in all the right places? Yep, green it is. I also love the halter silver beaded top, giving a little bit of bling to it.

After showering and doing my makeup, giving my eyes that smoky look, I decided to put my hair up in a French twist for a classy look. I thought it showcased my long slender neck and gave me that simple yet elegant look.

I picked out my favorite pair of earrings that my mother gave me for my twenty first birthday. They were long, chandelier, emerald and diamond earrings that just brushed my shoulders. I absolutely loved the way they gently kissed my lightly freckled shoulders.

I looked at the clock to see I only had fifteen minutes left before I had to leave. I hastily slid into my dress and grabbed my three inch silver stilettos and matching clutch. After one last glance in the mirror, I noticed I forgot to apply my lipstick. I dug into my clutch to find the perfect shade for tonight, going with the fuck me red lips. I smacked my lips after I was done spreading it on. Yep, I look good.

I stood at the top of the stairs waiting for my John to come. I noticed a few couples walking in, laughing and smiling at each other. For the first time in my life I thought to myself about what it would be like to actually be with the same person day in and day out; someone with whom I could share my life with. I quickly shook the thought away. Nah, that isn't for me. I love sex too much, and everyone says the sex stops after marriage. Hell, most of my Johns are married men if that doesn't tell you something.

I must have been lost in my thoughts because I didn't notice the sexy man trying to get my attention. "Scarlett?"

"Huh, oh, I'm sorry. My mind was somewhere else," I say with a small smile. I took a moment to really check my John out. Wow! He had to be at least 6'3, which is perfect since I'm 5'8 without my shoes on. I don't really have to look up to most men. He was slim but not too thin; more like he had a runner's figure or maybe he was a swimmer?

I couldn't help myself. He was wearing a very expensive tux that somehow gave him a truly regal look. I saw a slight smirk on his lips. "Like what you see?"

I looked up into his golden brown eyes and smiled. "Yes, yes I do." His eyes were the kindest eyes I have ever seen. I felt like I was going to drown in those murky depths.

John laughed, "Come on, Scarlett, let's get you inside." He held out the crook of his arm for me. I was giddy with excitement to slide my delicate hand into his arm. For some reason, an overwhelming feeling came over me. I felt proud. I felt strong like it was truly a gift to be on his arm.

I just couldn't understand why he needed to hire an escort. I can tell by the way everyone looked at him; he would have had no problems finding a date. "Ah, Mr. LaMar it is so good to see you again." I watched as this elderly man hastily shook my John's hand.

"I wouldn't have missed it for the world. You know how much I believe in this cause Mr. Black. Mr. Black may I introduce to you my lovely date for this evening? This lovely creature on my arm is Miss Scarlett. Miss Scarlett, this is Mr. Black, the owner of the museum and our host tonight for the fundraiser for foster kids."

I was shocked. I didn't know what the fundraiser was for, nor did I expect to be introduced to such an important man.

Before I had a chance to give Mr. Black my hand, he hook it himself and gently kissed my palm. "Miss Scarlett, may I say I am delighted to meet you, and you truly are a marvelous sight. There isn't a single piece of art in this building that can hold to your beauty." I couldn't help but blush at his praise.

"Thank you, Mr. Black. I'm overjoyed that Mr. LaMar brought me here tonight." I said sheepishly, as I took my hand back. Boy, it is a good thing I was able to pick up on the John's name. He forgot to tell me before we entered.

The evening flew by so fast that by time we were walking out of the museum it was going on eleven. I gave Mr. LaMar my sultry look and said, "Do you want to go back to my place?"

I watched as Mr. LaMar leaned into my hair and whispered in my ear. "Not this time but I want a rain check for the next time I see you." I wanted to do a happy dance right in front of him. He wanted to see me again, and he wasn't treating me like a prostitute.

Not able to stop myself, I smiled up at him. "As you wish, Mr. LaMar."

"Scarlett, you can call me Jake." Then he leaned down and placed the softest of kisses on my cheek. I was beyond shocked at the feeling of butterflies dancing in my belly just from his briefest of touches.

I couldn't help but look up into his caramel eyes. "As you wish, Jake." The night couldn't have been any better, so I turned around and walked away. Before I said or did something horrible.

And now, here I am writing to you and letting you know just how amazing my evening was with Mr. Jake LaMar. I have a feeling this is going to be one hell of a year.

January 2nd, 2014

    Ugh! What a freaking horrendous day. I had to have had the worst John ever tonight. Well, I should clarify he was the worst at first. As always Joe texted me earlier today with details where and when I was to meet my John. Well, today was no different than any other day, but my John was extremely obese. By the way, I have no problem with that. However, the problem I did have was the smell. This John smelled like he hadn't bathed in a few months.

    To be honest, the guy could have been kind of cute if he showered and shaved. Even his long beard, which hung down past his shoulders, had what looked like bits of food intertwined within. I knew from the start this was going to be tricky. Fortunately, we meet at a nice five star hotel which, by the looks of this guy, I couldn't figure out how he was able to afford it or me for that matter.

I was beyond grateful when I walked into the room and saw a huge hot tub with a lot of girly products on the edge. I quickly turned on my charm and prayed he didn't figure out what I was up to. I seductively walked over to the beautiful white porcelain tub and turned it on. Then I hastily opened up the petite bottle of bath oil and dumped it all in.

The room instantly smelled a little spicy. I liked it. I turned around to look at my John while I let the water run. While sitting on the edge of the tub, I slipped my wedge sandals off my feet. Then slowly I removed my tank top and short jean skirt, leaving me in nothing but my black lace bra and matching boy shorts. I was extremely giddy to see my John's eyes get as big as saucers. The only thing going through my mind at that moment was good now I can clean him before we do anything. I know, it was wrong of me to think like that, but I just don't have the stomach for it.

"Come here," I purred to him. I watched amazed at how fast he was able to remove all of his clothing and had them tossed in just about every direction of the room. I watched him move as he watched me. His dull grey eyes were trained solely on me. I unclasped my front clasp bra and let my perfectly proportioned D cup breasts out to breathe.

Then, I slowly removed my panties and gently tossed them aside.

As I stepped into the hot oily water, I grabbed the washcloth that was shaped like a swan and brought it into the soothing pool with me. I looked up to see my John standing over the tub looking down at me hungrily. I dunked the cloth into the water releasing the swan then seductively moved it between my long legs and up my flat belly. "Are you going to join me or just stand there watching me?"

He grunted then stepped into the tub. I guess he wasn't much for words. As he stepped in, he turned around so that he was sitting in between my legs. As he sat down, an overflow of water splashed out of the tub and onto the floor. I quickly worked my magic. With my washcloth in my hand, I started to rub his back. Once clean, I placed tender kisses on his now smooth skin. Then, I moved my hands under his arms and started to scrub his broad chest. "That feels good."

I smiled. That was the first real sentence he had said all night. "I'm glad you are enjoying it. May I ask you a question?" I noticed him stiffen at my words.

"Sure."

"What is your name?" I figured I had to start small with this man of few words. I heard him take a deep breath and relax at my question.

"My name is James, but some people call me Jim or Jimmy." I couldn't help but smile at this man. Once clean, he didn't seem all too bad. I couldn't figure out why anyone would let themselves get that bad. Was it just laziness?

"Well James, is it okay that I call you James?" He nodded so I went on. "My name is Scarlett, but you probably already know that. I hope to take good care of you today. Would you like me to wash your hair for you?" I heard him grunt then nod his head. James seemed to be enjoying the bath, so I couldn't figure out why he wasn't cleaned beforehand.

I reached with my toes and grabbed the nozzle of the tub, which was on a longer hose, and pulled it into reaching distance of my free hand. "Okay. Turn the water on to the temp you want, and I'll get started."

As I watched him lean forward, I noticed his hair was also very long like his beard as if it too hasn't been cut in a long time. It also looked very dull and unhealthy. I couldn't help but wonder what this man had gone through. Whatever it was, it must have been a rough ride.

James handed me the nozzle, and I quickly went to work washing his long hair. By the time I was through, the water was dark and dirty but his hair and skin was nice and clean. I stepped up and climbed out, letting James drain the tub. I grabbed the bigger swan and unfolded it so I had a towel. As I dried my body, I looked over at James and saw him just watching me.

His eyes were now sparkling, and he looked almost like a brand new man. I smiled up at him. "You're looking good, James." For the first time that night I saw him smile.

"Thank you, Scarlett. It has been a very long time anyone has taken care of me." I really didn't know what to say to that, so I just nodded.

"Well, come on now. I have more work to do." I reached my pruney hand out to him and watched as he engulfed it with his own. As he stood, I took a good long look at him. Yes, he was bigger all around then what I'm use to, but he also was much bigger were it counted too. "Come here, big guy." I then lead him to the king size bed.

I knew that men that paid for escorts expect the escort to do all the work, and really my job is to get it going. Most men will end up doing what they want in the end. James and I only had an hour left, so I was going to make sure he got his money worth at least. I gently pushed him on the bed so he was sitting on the edge while I knelt in between his massive legs.

While looking straight at his engorged penis, I started to salivate. Yep, you got it. I'm one of those girls. I love dick! I took my slender hand and wrapped it around his hard shaft. I smiled when I heard a gasp come out of James's mouth. I continued to stroke him and then decided to add some tongue and suction into the mix. With my other hand, I cupped his hefty balls and started to delicately play with them.

I pumped him with my right hand. Every time I moved my hand up, I made sure to put more pressure on the tip of his head with my lips. When I moved my hand back down, I lapped at the underside of his head. James started to moan. I watched and knew all the signs. He was going to come soon. But, this wasn't the way I wanted it to happen.

I abruptly stopped and got to my feet. James was gawking at me in awe and wonder. I pushed him all the way back so that he was now flat on the bed. "Do you want me?" I purred out.

"Yes," was his only reply. That was all I needed to know before I moved on.

"Let me know if you want anything different." I watched as he nodded. Then, I got up and straddled his waist and plunged down on his massive erection. James and I gasped at the same time. I don't know if I have ever felt so full from just one man before. Once my body was fully adjusted to his size, I began to ride.

I was beyond ecstatic at all the feeling erupting through me. Every time I dropped down to his hilt, I was hitting my G-spot. I kept going until I exploded all over him. I mean I have had a female ejaculation before, but it has been years and never like this.

I couldn't control my feeling and locked eyes with James as I came. I don't think by the look in his eyes that James has ever had that happen to him before. I smiled down at him. Then, out of nowhere I was tossed like a rag doll onto my back.

The wind was knocked out of me momentary. By the time I was able to control myself again, I found James now standing between my legs. I opened up more to him exposing my most vulnerable area. I watched in amazement as he guided his rock hard cock into me.

This new position didn't exactly hit my G-spot, but it still felt completely amazing. I arched my back up giving him more access. I can still feel, at this moment, the way his hands cupped my hips, pulling me closer to him with every thrust he gave me.

I watched with excitement as he pulled out not knowing what he was going to do next. I was hastily tossed onto my belly. I felt his finger enter me and then out again, lapping all my juices. Then, I really got excited when I notice what he had planned. I felt a gentle brush of moisture at my back door. I arched more into him, letting him know I wanted this too.

With a couple more laps of moisture, he carefully pushed his finger in. My God it felt amazing. Slowly, he moved in and out and began to stretch me. When I was finally were he wanted me, I was a little nervous to have something so big going in my out hole, but I was also giddy with anticipation.

I did the best that I could and relaxed all of my muscles, and then he was in. I let out a breath of air I didn't realize I was holding in and waited for him to move. James moved slowly at first and then started to pound into me. I couldn't contain the screams of joy that were flowing out of me.

I was having some kind of emotional overload and began panting. I knew within moments I was going to come again. Then, with his right hand he started to rub and massage my clit sending me over the edge.

If the neighbors didn't hear me scream before, I'm sure there is no way they didn't hear me now. With a few more spasms rolling through my body I was spent. Luckily for me, James came at the same time I did. I looked at the clock to see how much time he had left and saw it was five till.

I felt exhausted but in such a good way. It's strange just how different this night turned out from what I was expecting. I rolled off the bed and started to get dressed. Once I found all my clothing and had put myself back in order, I looked one last time at James. "Thanks for an amazing night James. I truly hope to see you again."

I watched as James panted and smiled up at me. Not just one of those little smiles but an amazingly huge smile. I couldn't help myself but to smile back at him. For some reason I hoped I would see him again. I just hope next time he is a little cleaner to begin with.

That was how I left him tonight. Just lying in bed with a huge smile plastered on his face, knowing I'm the one that did that for him gave me a thrill like no other.

January 3rd, 2014

Today was one of those days that weren't quite bad but not that fantastic either. This doesn't happen often, but it obviously does happen. I had two Johns today, and yes, they were at the same time. Now, I don't usually mind taking on two men. Really, more the merrier if you ask me.

The only problem I had with my Johns tonight was the fact that they were homosexual. Like I said, it doesn't happen often, but there are times when gay men want to see what it is like to try the opposite sex. I don't have a problem with homosexuals at all. However, I'm in this job for the sex as I have already stated. If you're truly gay you aren't going to want to get it on with a girl no matter what.

I guess what I'm trying to say here is that I felt a little left out. The sex started out okay; maybe a little awkward on their part. I can tell from the beginning that they were both nervous. I did the best I could to calm their fears and went as slow as I could.

I started with the more dominate male, caressing his cock through his tight designer jeans. I was expecting it to take a little effort for him to get aroused, but I was mistaken. He was all ready to go. He reminded me of a knight ready to fight; tall and strong and ready to ride. I guess I was also mistaken on his fear. Maybe he was just worried about what his partner would think?

Knowing that he was the more dominate one, I had to order the submissive into place. I looked at his partner, seeing him shake just slightly. "Come here." I told him in a gentle voice. "I want you to unbutton his shirt. While I let him help his partner undress, I took care of his belt and shoved down his jeans; happy to see he was going commando.

His cock was standard in size, but it sure sprung out of those jeans like it had a mind of its own. I looked up and noticed his partner was done unbuttoning his shirt and was now just watching me. "Get undressed and join me." He hesitated at first but then started taking his clothes off.

While he was getting undressed, I started to massage the dominate's balls and scrotum. I started to lightly kiss his heavy sack with the tips of my fingers, teasing him and making him want more but not giving in to his desire.

Soon, his partner joined me quickly, grabbing his cock and started to suck and play. I was happy to see he seemed to overcome his fear of me. I began to suck his sack and twirled my tongue around his heavy balls. I enjoyed the light moans pouring out of this throat.

I got up and moved over to the bed, lying down so my head was hanging off the edge. I watched as the more dominate one moved away from his partner and came over to me. He knew exactly what I wanted him to do. I leaned my head back and opened my mouth as big as I could while he plunged into me almost causing me to gag in the process.

With this angle, I was truly able to deep throat him and at the same time watch his partner come up behind him. I felt the more dominate one bend over me more. He started to lick my clit. I bucked and moaned with pleasure. While he was bent over playing with me, his partner had the perfect view to start playing with his anus. I was able to hear the sounds of lapping and spitting. I was pretty sure he was getting his "friend" ready.

For some reason this really turned me on, and my juices started to flow. I decided I wanted to join in on the fun and pulled back, rotating my body so that I was now aligned with the more dominates shaft. I grabbed his cock and slowly guided it into my sweet wet folds. I looked up to see his green eyes boring into me. I could hear his breathing become more labored as he slowly moved in and out of me.

I then noticed him stiffen as his partner decided to take that moment to enter in behind him. *Oh hell.* I couldn't believe I was getting so turned on by this. Once he was relaxed again, I was able to feel his shift in desire. He began to move in a more frantic pace; pounding into me and giving me everything he had to give. It was surreal to me feeling both him and his partner move like one engine.

Suddenly, they both stopped at the same time, and his partner moved out out him. I noticed that somehow, without speaking to each other, they both decided it was time to change. At that moment, I decided I was wrong yet again. I don't think I was with the more dominating after all. This one had caramelized brown eyes, and his cock was impressive. Not James impressive but he was well endowed.

I was even more excited at this revolution. He picked my hips up like I weighed nothing at all and brought them to his soft lips. I started to feel tingles running through my body as soon as he started to suck up my creamy honey. I was beginning to think that this man had to have been with a woman once before. There is no way he was able to pleasure me without knowing what to do.

Hell, green eyes didn't really do anything but lick. He never once played with my nipples or anything. This brown eyed stallion had nothing holding him back. I bucked as he plunged two fingers into my tight sheath. I was in bliss that I didn't have a clue what green eyes was doing. All I knew is that I was actually really enjoying myself.

Then, just like that, it all went downhill. Brown eyes stopped paying attention to me and started paying attention to his partner. Now, like I said, I'm not bothered by them being gay. But I was disappointed. I truly wanted some hot sex here. Once those two got started, I was completely forgotten. I did end up leaving with my money, but I wasn't exactly satisfied if you know what I mean.

So...yep that was my night. Not the best but I guess it could have been better. Well, at least I have my trusty rabbit vibrator to help me out tonight. Can you hear the sarcasm there? Well, it's better than nothing at all.

January 4th, 2014

Today was my day off, so I decided to spend my free time cleaning my apartment and running errands. While I was out, I ran into Jake. I couldn't believe it. I was lost in my own little world while at the local grocery store.

Yep, I was so engrossed in what I was doing that I had no clue I was being followed. I was startled when I was looking at the feminine deodorant spray. I can laugh about it now, but I was so embarrassed that I was caught with a bottle of Summer's Eve in my hand. Jake came up from behind me and whispered in my ear as I was leaning over the display, "I don't think you need that." I ended up jumping up and hit him in the nose. The bottle I was holding went flying and hit some poor bystander in the head.

I spun around on him and poked my finger in his chest. "Don't you ever do that to me again!" I gasped out. I was actually having a difficult time controlling my breathing. When I was finally able to calm down my emotions, I looked up to see Jake had a shit eating grin on his face. I smacked him in the upper arm. "This is not funny. What are you doing here anyways?"

"Same as you I suppose," he said while laughing. "Although, I don't need the feminine spray either." I didn't know what I wanted to do more, run or beat the hell out of his handsome face. I ended up stomping my foot and tried to walk away. Before I got too far, Jake grabbed my arm. "Wait! I'm sorry. I didn't truly mean to scare you. I just couldn't resist. I had to talk to you again."

I turned around and looked into his chocolate murky eyes. I really couldn't tell what he was thinking. I tried my best to relax and give him the benefit of the doubt. "Listen, I am sorry. I just wanted to talk to you. Do you have any plans for tonight?"

That stopped me cold. I was now beyond pissed. "Listen here. If you want to set up a date then you have to go through Joe. I'm telling you this now. It isn't going to happen tonight. I'm taking the night off." I began to turn again, trying to escape this infuriating man. How dare he think it was okay to plan a date without speaking to Joe? My arm was grabbed once more. I turned once again and snarled, "Let go of me."

"No." Jake said in a calm voice.

If people could see my face now I probably had smoke coming out of my nostrils. "LET. GO. OF. ME." I couldn't believe in the audacity of this guy. How on Earth did I ever think he was charming?

"Listen, I'm sorry Scarlett. I just wanted to ask you out on a real date. I didn't mean to upset you. I just wanted to get the chance to know the real Scarlett." I felt like my mind was caught in a tornado spiraling out of control. I didn't know what to think or say. Maybe I should give him a chance. Hell, I can't. He is a client. I can't date a client for crying out loud.

With my mind set on what I was going to do, I looked back up at him. "Jake, I really don't think..."

I was cut off by his long finger pressing up against my lips. "Scarlett, it's just one date. Will you please join me for dinner? I promise that if you don't have a good time you won't have to see me again." He removed his finger from my lips. It is true what he said; if I don't want to see him again, I don't have to. What do I really have to lose?

"Okay," I said hesitantly. "I'll go out to dinner with you. But, just this once."

Jake smiled, "I'll take it. What time can I pick you up?"

Oh, I knew better than that one. Rule number one: you never let a stranger know where you live. "I'll meet you there. Just tell me where and when."

Jake must have figured I wasn't going to budge on this one. "Okay, how about we meet at my place at seven?"

I nodded, "Okay, your place it is. I just need the address." After I was given his address, I decided it was time for me to get out of this store. I guess I had a date to get ready for.

I ended up being fashionably late like every girl on a date should be. I learned at a young age that if you make a man wait on you, when you finally show up they end up being putty in your hands. Or at least it worked on high school guys. Jake didn't seem to notice.

In fact, he didn't seem to notice anything about me tonight. I wore a short black sleeveless dress with red fuck me heels. I even curled my hair so long ringlets spiraled down my back. I knew I looked good, but Jake didn't say anything. All he said when I got there was, "Come in and have a seat at the table. Dinner will be ready shortly." Did I have lipstick on my teeth or something? I don't think I have ever been treated like I was truly there. I was always told how beautiful I was.

All it did was get me thinking. *Maybe I should say something first.* I mean, after all, he did look amazingly sexy in his Calvin Klein gray suit. He wasn't wearing a tie for me to grab onto, but he did have the first few buttons of his dress shirt undone, giving him that "I'm sexy and I know it" look. It also showcased a part of his chest, letting me know he either shaved or waxed the hair. Now, that was hot as fuck.

I couldn't stop myself even if I wanted to. I licked my lips, and all I wanted to do was run my hands up under his shirt and caress the smooth tight skin underneath. Oh hell, let's be honest here. I wanted to do a hell of a lot more than caress his chest. I looked around and noticed that everything seemed to perfect. Nothing was out of place. It was just so clean. I wonder if he has a housekeeper or something.

So, I figured what the hell. He wasn't saying anything, so I might as well be. "I like your place." Shit that was pretty lame to start a conversation with. God, I felt so stupid.

Jake turned to look at me then stopped like he finally looked at me. Do you know what I mean? "Um, thanks. I like keeping my place in order. It makes me feel in control." Huh, I wonder what exactly that means. Is Jake one of those control freaks?

"Well, it looks very nice. So, what's for dinner anyways?" I just need to get off that conversation.

"Oh, it's nothing really special. Just lasagna and I made a cheesecake for dessert." *Yum, cheesecake*. I wonder what kind it is.

"That sounds amazing. I can't believe you made all of this." I looked around at the table set for two. It was perfect. It was just what you would see in a movie, a long stem candle sat in the middle, flickering here and there giving it that romantic vibe.

Even the china was beautiful and delicate. It looked like bone china with a silver rim around the outer edge; simply stunning if you ask me. Jake placed a small portion of lasagna on my plate and a piece on his. It looked and smelled heavenly. "Thank you. This looks incredible."

"It's my pleasure," he said as he took his seat and began to eat. So far it was pretty lousy conversation. "So Scarlett, tell me a little about you."

I looked up right before I placed a heaping forkful of noodles and cheese into my mouth. "What would you like to know? There really isn't much to tell."

He smiled at that, "I would love to know everything about you, your thoughts, why you became an escort, your dreams, everything."

"Wow! Okay, at the moment I'm thinking this has to be the best damn lasagna I have ever had."

Jake laughed, and it was one of those curl your toes kinds of laugh where his whole face lit up with joy. "Oh Scarlett, you have no idea do you?" I shook my head not understanding. Jake leaned back and grabbed some kind of cardboard off the kitchen counter. He flipped it around so I could look.

I couldn't help myself, and I started to laugh too. He was holding one of those frozen premade lasagna boxes where all you have to do is pop it in the oven and there you go. "Well, it is very good. You did an amazing job heating it up."

I picked up the wine glass in front of me and took a small sip because I'm not a big wine fan, but I didn't want to upset him. I was rather surprised at the sweet sparkling liquid inside. "What kind of wine is this?"

"Oh, that is Mosco De'Ausie. Do you like it?"

I looked up into his muddy brown eyes and smiled, "Yes, very much so."

"I'm glad. Now, please tell me why you decided to become an escort." I swallowed more of the sweet ambrosia before I began.

"I guess it was just a very easy decision for me. I lost my V-card when I was a freshman in high school. I guess you could have called me boy crazy. I fell in love with sex. Yes, I mean I love sex every way shape and form. I just couldn't get enough of it, so that is why I decided to become an escort. What better way to live my life but by doing the thing I love to do most? And, I get paid a hell of a lot of money."

Jake smiled at me, "So I take it you love sex." I chucked a small piece of garlic bread at him. He caught it and tossed it into his mouth, smiling the whole time. I couldn't help but smile back. *That jerk.*

"What about you?"

"What about me? Do I love sex? Well, hell yeah. What man doesn't?" I laughed at him but was happy to hear that he loved sex too. I couldn't figure out why he didn't want it on New Year's Day when he paid for it.

"Well, what do you do for a living then? I can see by looking around you are very wealthy man." I watched as he raised his eyebrow to that.

"Yes and no. I'm a stock broker, but really I don't make all that much money. Most of the money and items you see here are from my parent's inheritance. I lost both my parents on 9/11." I looked up shocked.

"Where they in the towers when the plane crashed?" I was horrified to think about that day. I remembered it clearly. I was already at school when we got the announcement of the attack on the twin towers. I was in English class at the moment which, by the way, was my worst class. Anyways, I remember Mrs. Hammond turning on the class TV to broadcast the towers. By time we got to see the towers, both of them were hit but hadn't fallen yet. I remembered the feelings rushing through me as I watched in horror as the towers fell: helplessness, dread, pain, worry, lost. Everything I thought of America being a safe country was torn away from me in a blink of an eye.

Jake tore me away from my memory, "No, my parents were on the first plane that crashed."

I reached out and grabbed his hand. "Jake, I'm so sorry for your loss. That truly must have been a horrible way for your parents to go."

"It was," was all he said. But what more could he say?

"I'm sorry I asked." As I gave his hand a gentle squeeze. Hell, now I brought this dinner to a dreadful mood. I just need to change the subject. "How about that cheesecake?"

Jake smile, "Sure thing." I watched as he slowly got to his feet and started to get to work on placing two pieces of cheesecake on to two dessert plates.

As he handed me my plate, I noticed that the cheesecake was like nothing I have seen before. "Wow, this looks incredible. What kind is it?" The cheesecake was a creamy cheese color mixed with a bright lime green intertwined within.

"It's called Key Lime Pie Cheesecake. It's one of my favorites." I looked up to see such joy on his face as he almost lovingly stroked his fork through the end. You could see such love and pride in his work.

I took such a small slice of the end, not wanting to look like a freaking pig even though I just wanted to plunge my whole face into it. Yep, I love cheesecake that much. As I placed the piece on my tongue, I swear I was about to have an orgasm. It was perfect; sweet but not too sweet and creamy by the way it just melted on your tongue. The taste of lime made my saliva glands dance with pleasure.

I looked up to see Jake watching me with amusement. "What? Do I have something on my face?"

He laughed and shook his head, "No, but just that look says it all. I want to always see that look of pure pleasure on your face." I blushed at his kind words not knowing what to say to that. Before I knew it, the cake was gone. I really wanted more but knew I couldn't act like a total hog.

"This cheesecake is the best. Please tell me you didn't buy this too?"

Jake laughed again, "No, this I did actually make. I make a few different cheesecakes, but this one and my chocolate chip one are my favorite."

"Wow, I bet you can make a lot of money selling these. I know I would probably buy one a week. I'd also get fat if you do, but, my God, it is heavenly."

Jake busted out laughing so hard he started to tear up some. I don't know if I ever remember anyone enjoying something I said so much. "I'm just pleased you enjoy it. I tell you what; whenever you want a cheesecake, I'll be more than happy to make one for you on one condition."

"What's that?"

"You have to eat it in front of me. I just love your beautiful intoxicating facial expressions." I blushed again like I was some little school girl with a crush. I shook that thought away.

"You have got yourself a deal." Even though I knew this couldn't last. There is no way I can have a relationship and be an escort. It just can't happen. Can it? I watched as Jake leaned over the table and and wiped away some cheesecake I must of had at the corner of my lips. I watched him with hunger as he guided the small crumb into his juicy lips.

I couldn't take it anymore. I wanted him, and I wanted him NOW. I stood and sauntered over to him. I knew by the look in his eyes that he also knew what I was doing. He pushed his chair out, giving me room to straddle his lap.

I didn't waste anytime and began to kiss him feverously. My God, he sure could kiss. It has been a long time since I have been kissed. That is one of the rules when I'm on the job: No kissing. But, now I couldn't stop myself even if I wanted to. Without taking a breath, I removed his jacket and began to finish unbuttoning his dress shirt. I didn't even notice, until his hands were on my nipples, that he had pulled my strapless dress down. I moaned with excitement and anticipation.

I arched my body into his hands, letting him know I wanted and needed his touch. I broke the kiss and began to pant. I locked eyes with Jake, and I knew our eyes were mirroring each other. We both wanted and needed this connection.

I knew by the look in his eyes this wasn't going to be long and tender. Hell, I didn't want that anyways. I stood up giving me access to his fly. I hastily unzipped his pants and released his hard cock. I was a little saddened to see that he really didn't have much there, but I could work with it without a problem.

I was thankful that I had decided not to wear panties today and began to guide his shaft into my hungry pussy. Straddling him once more, I began to ride hard and fast using the back of the chair as an anchor. I really wasn't feeling all that much downstairs, but as soon as Jake's long slender tongue started to tease my nipple that was all it took. I leaned back and thrust my tits into his face, wanting and needing more.

At one point, Jake bit down on righty giving me just the right amount of pain with pleasure which was all it took for me to cum. As my body began to come down from the high, Jake came soon after.

I noticed then that Jake was looking at me like I was his cheesecake where I felt like it was just you know...okay. At that moment, I knew I needed to leave. I got up and readjusted my dress. "I'm sorry Jake, but I need to go."

"Are you sure?" The look of panic on his face was killing me.

"I'm sorry, but yes. I have a busy day tomorrow. Thank you so much for a wonderful evening." Without another look I walked out the door.

That was just over an hour ago when I left, and I still don't know what to truly think or do. Jake does seem like a great guy, and I know I wanted him. There just wasn't much that did it for me in the sex department, and as you know, I need sex...A LOT. I guess this is just something I will have to think about. What do I want? I mean, he is an amazing man who is rich, sexy, smart, and well, I can't forget, an amazing baker. I love cheesecake. What am I going to do?

To be continued....

About the Author

Kristin Michelle Adams lives in Northwest Indiana with her loving husband Derrick. She has been suffering with a learning disability all of her life, but loves to do the best that she can in writing. She lives with her three Beagles and two cats. Kristin is also an avid reader and reads about a book a day. Her favorite authors are Richelle Mead, Kristin Secorsky, Karen Marie Moning, Olivia Cunning, Luke Young, and the list keeps going.

Books by Kristin Michelle Adams in reading order.

Temptations Series

Connor

Woody

Riley

Jack Hammer

Hunter

Tara

Stand alone

Hard As Steel

Hard As Steel

Prologue

Stories have been passed down from generation to generation; that just over a thousand years ago men and women did coexist together. I'm not sure if this is actually true or not, as I have only been around for twenty five years. As the story goes, men and women couldn't control their sexual desires, or be smart enough to have protected sex. So disease spread all over the world, killing off people by the thousands. So the government thought it necessary to separate men and women to save the human race. Over a thousand years has passed since the government separated the men and women. The only human males I have ever seen are babies.

Let me explain the current age of the human race. When women reach the age of twenty five, we go to the government facility to pick a sex bot. Rather than be artificially inseminated with male sperm that is clean of all disease, injected into the womb in a hospital like they used to. The government stepped in deciding that males and females should be completely separated. They then created the sex bots which collect sperm specimens from the men, and are cryogenically frozen until the time they are needed to impregnate the women. This is how reproduction is controlled without the actual human male contacting the female or vise versa. When a male baby is born, it stays with its mother until the age of two and is then sent off to live with the men.

Chapter 1 Infinity

Today is my birthday, which means it will be the first time I actually interact with a sex bot. I'm excited to pick out which bot is going to be mine for the rest of my life. Will I pick a sex bot with blonde hair and green eyes, like my mother did, or will I pick out a dark haired, blue or brown eyed bot? I don't know? I have been thinking of this for years now, and still haven't figured out what type of bot I would prefer. I was told that whatever choice you pick, will relate to the actual male human that the sperm belongs to. So that would mean that my real father possibly had blonde hair and green eyes. Because I have sandy blonde hair and green eyes, and my mother has blue eyes and auburn colored hair. I arrived at the facility, and the waiting room seemed too quiet for me. It was as though the stillness only made me more anxious. I couldn't stop my knee from bouncing up and down, I was so nervous. My mom had explained to me basically what to expect. But still, how will I know if I'm picking the right one?

"Infinity" The nurse called, she was quite normal with red hair and blue eyes peering out of the open door at me. I jumped up, and walked towards her while keeping my head down.

"Are you ready to pick out your bot?" The nurse asked me.

"I don't know, to be honest with you. I'm not really sure what I want." I spoke the words I was thinking.

The nurse patted my hand. "That's alright honey, they never do."

We walked into a huge room filled with nothing but rows and rows of sex bots, in every height, race, and body type possible. At that moment all I knew for sure was; I didn't want a short man. So I skipped the first two rows completely because they were all my height or shorter.

"Do the heights reflect the human men they were made from?" I had to know, because I knew I wanted a better chance at a tall child.

"Yes they do." The nurse replied.

"Good." Was all I could think to say, as I stared in awe at all the bots.

I walked down the third row and started with the blondes. Nothing caught my eye, so I continued down the next row with light brown hair. Nope: nothing. I thought. Finally on the 4th row I was about a quarter of the way down when I stopped in my tracks. The bot I was looking at has medium length chestnut brown hair, with the lightest blue eyes I have ever seen. The tag on him read: Asher.

"Asher, step forward." I commanded and the bot took a step forward as I looked him over. He was dressed like all the rest in a military fashion of combat boots and black cargo pants, with a t-shirt. Asher looked to be around 6'2 or 6'3 which would be perfect to my 5'9 height. I walked slowly around taking him in.

"Asher, take off your shirt." I commanded. The robot moved slowly and removed his shirt.

I don't know what it was but, I could tell right away this was the one. My body was already reacting with excitement. Asher had rock hard abs and perfect pecs. I rubbed my hands up his body feeling his warm skin under my fingers. I looked down at his waist and groin out of sheer curiosity. There I saw something growing larger in his pants. I giggled not realizing that was going to happen if I touched him.

I backed up. "Asher you can put your shirt back on now." I tried to keep the command in my voice but I was shocked, nervous, and fidgety at the moment.

Asher slowly bent forward and picked up his t-shirt and put it back on. My goodness he had a very nice ass too. I mused, and I couldn't help but smack it while he was bent over. I was surprised when he stumbled slightly. Huh, I thought. I had never seen Todd stumble before when mom had done that. It must be an added humanity trait to the newer model. Todd (dad I guess you can call him) is an X-Bot 2000. Asher here is the upgraded version X-Bot 3000.

"Asher, follow me."I commanded, walking back toward the nurse's station becoming very nervous for the next step.

"Ah, looks like you picked a good one." The nurse suggested, trying to ease me.

I turned and looked up at Asher, smiling. "I hope I did. And uh, I guess I'm ready to take him for a test ride."

The nurse laughed as she replied. "Follow me." I followed the nurse to a room just down the hall. There wasn't much to the room other than a queen sized bed.

"Here you are Hun, just press this button here. (She pointed to a red button on the wall next to the door), when you are done." She winked as she said it.

"Okay I will." I nodded at the nurse as she left the room.

I walked in the room with Asher following. "Asher, close the door."

I started to unbutton my shirt with shaky hands. I don't understand why I'm so nervous, it's not like Asher is going to care what I look like he's a bot. He has no real thought or feeling. Asher turned, stopped, and stared at me. Well, that isn't creepy at all. I thought as I dropped my shirt on the floor, leaving me in my jeans and bra alone.

"Asher, get undressed." I commanded, and I swear it looked like he hesitated for a moment. Wow, these upgrades are amazing, and so life like. I dropped my pants and panties, then unclasped my bra and left it in the pile on the floor. I looked up to see Asher naked and his cock growing larger while he stared at me. "Wow! How big does it get? Do I want it any bigger?" I blurted out. No, there is no way that is going to fit inside of me I concluded mentally.

"Come here Asher." I said with a shaky voice.